THE WoLF'S CoLoURFUL COAT

Avril McDonald

Illustrated by Tatiana Minina

Crown House Publishing Limited
www.crownhouse.co.uk

First published by

Crown House Publishing Ltd
Crown Buildings, Bancyfelin, Carmarthen, Wales, SA33 5ND, UK
www.crownhouse.co.uk

and

Crown House Publishing Company LLC
PO Box 2223, Williston, VT 05495, USA
www.crownhousepublishing.com

Illustrations by Tatiana Minina

British Library Cataloguing-in-Publication Data
A catalogue entry for this book is available from the British Library.

Print ISBN: 978-178583020-4
Mobi ISBN: 978-178583080-8
ePub ISBN: 978-178583081-5
ePDF ISBN: 978-178583082-2

LCCN 2015953332

Printed and bound in the UK by
Gomer Press, Llandysul, Ceredigion

Because kindness and love can reveal greatness.

Thanks to Åsa Pettersson for her contribution to Feel Brave's work, to the poet Robert Saxton for his editorial directive and to Jill Duncan and Yemma Barsanti for their creative wisdom.

Deep in the forest
the fairies were told
That winter was coming
and bringing the cold.

The streams would freeze over.
Wild winds would blow
And the ground would be covered
in white fluffy snow.

They whispered the news to Wise Owl
who then flew,
To tell the whole forest,
so everyone knew.

Catreen wasn't pleased.
    She just liked the hot sun.
She didn't think winter
    was very much fun,

With wet soggy socks
    and big heavy clothes,
Cold hands and cold feet
    and a red Rudolph nose.

But Wolfgang longed for
     the cold and the wet:
He had a new coat
     that he hadn't worn yet.

This colourful coat
     was bright orange and blue
With pink stripes and dots –
     he had matching boots too!

His grandma had made it
     with love and great care.
It just hadn't been cold enough
     for him to wear.

But now with cold winds
     and fresh snow on the way,
He put on his coat
     and he skipped off to play.

As he happily whistled
his favourite song,
A dog, two racoons
and a rat came along.

Something about them
made Wolfgang feel bad:
The racoons seemed okay
but the dog looked quite mad.

And the rat ... well,
    he simply looked rather mean,
But his nose was quite cute,
    like a pink jelly bean.

The dog growled at Wolfgang,
"You look like a clown!
That's a girl's coat you're wearing."
He pushed Wolfgang down.

And the rat threw a snowball
that hit him in the eye.
The racoons laughed out loud
as he tried not to cry.

After they'd gone,
brushing snow off his face,

He crept back to the tree house,
his favourite place.

And he didn't come out,
he just stayed safe inside –
The tree house was always
a good place to hide.

Wolfgang was much too afraid
to go out,
Just in case the mad dog
and the rat were about.

But the tree house got boring ...
    and after a while,
Spider crept down:
    she missed Wolfgang's smile.

"Oh Wolfgang," said Spider,
    "don't hide on your own.
I know what they said
    made you feel you're alone.

But your coat is not why
    they were being unkind:
They would have upset
    anyone they could find.

Some of us who
    have been hurt by someone
Might think that to hurt
    is the way things are done.

And some are unkind
    and make others feel bad
When they simply don't know
    what it's like to feel sad.

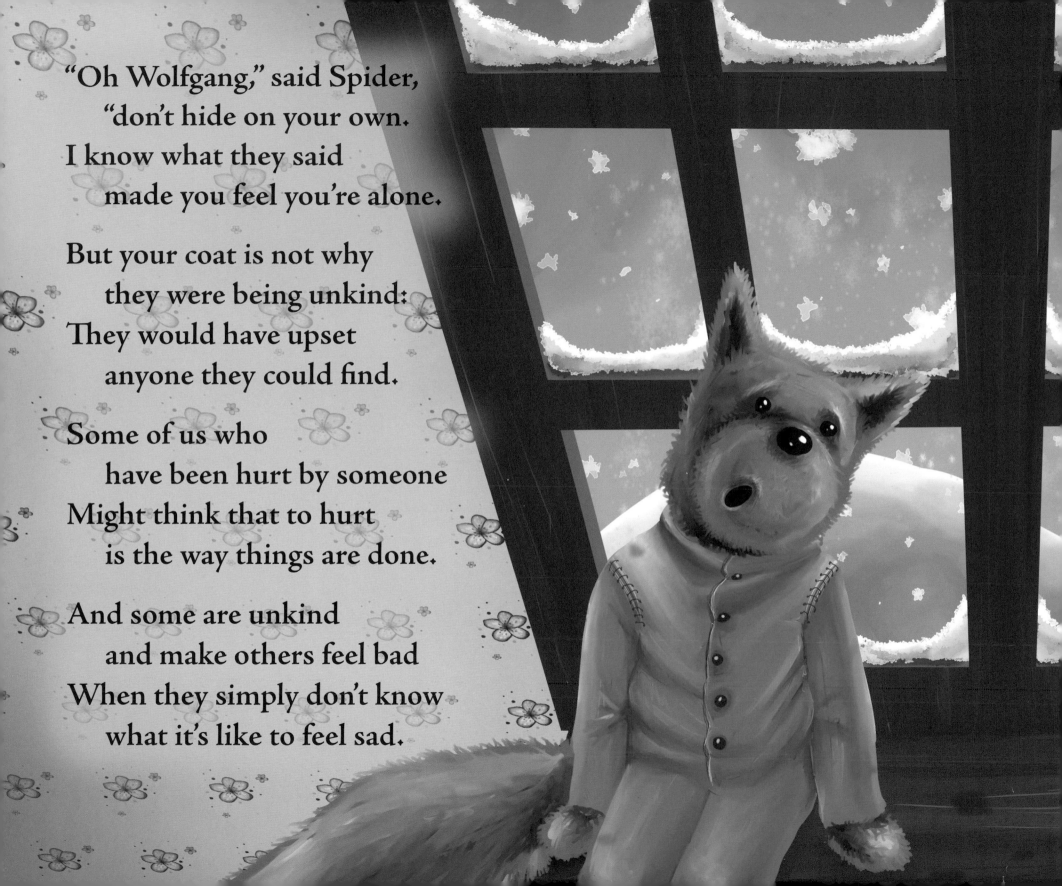

What they need is more love,
    so the best thing to do
Is be kind, brave and strong …
    most of all just be you!

Tell someone you trust
    that you're feeling this way –
Like Wise Owl, who's clever
    and knows what to say.

Your friends are down there.
    You've been missed. Can't you tell?
Look, they're all wearing
    colourful coats as well."

Wolfgang looked down
from the window to see
His friends making snow angels
under the tree.

He told Wise Owl
that he still felt quite scared,
Though not so much now
that his problem was shared ...

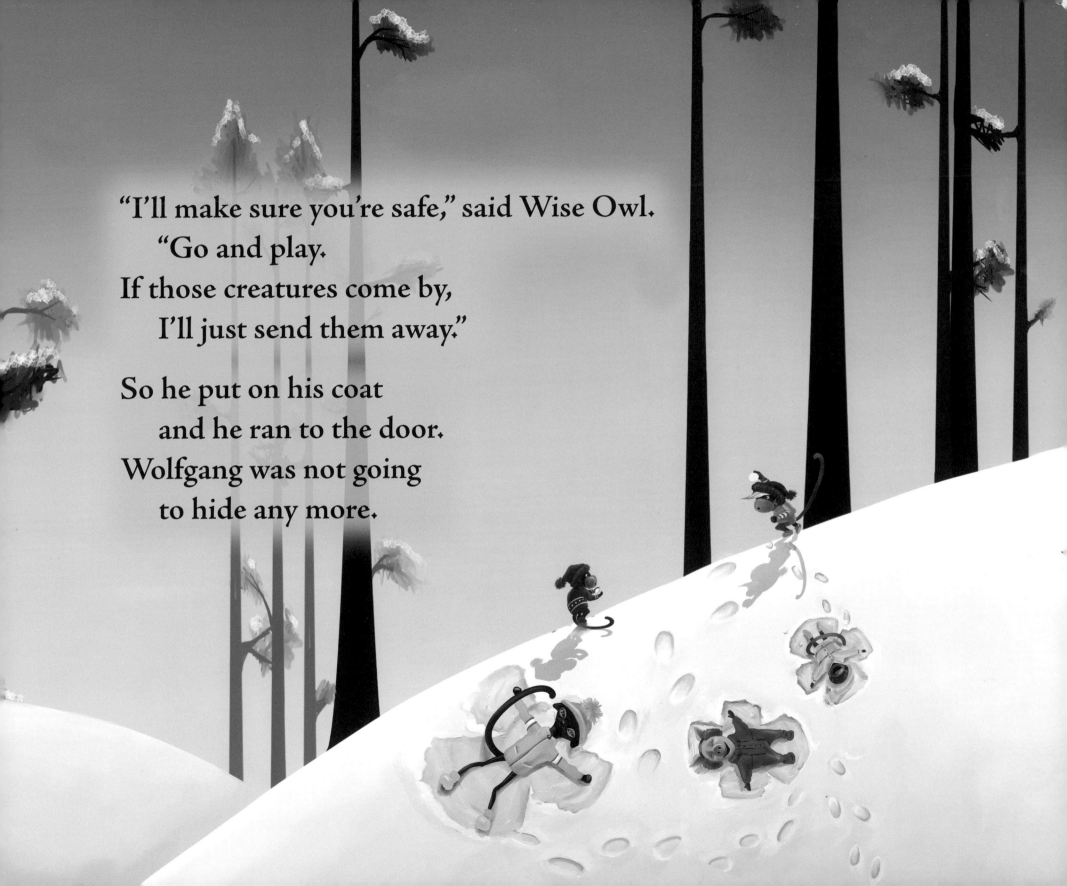

"I'll make sure you're safe," said Wise Owl.
    "Go and play.
If those creatures come by,
    I'll just send them away."

So he put on his coat
    and he ran to the door.
Wolfgang was not going
    to hide any more.

Days and weeks passed.
   They had wonderful fun,
Building grand snowmen
   in crisp winter sun.

Then one day they happened
   to play hide and seek,
Which, whatever the weather,
   they played twice a week.

As Wolfgang was hiding,
he heard a strange sound:
Ice cracking, and splashing
and crashing around.

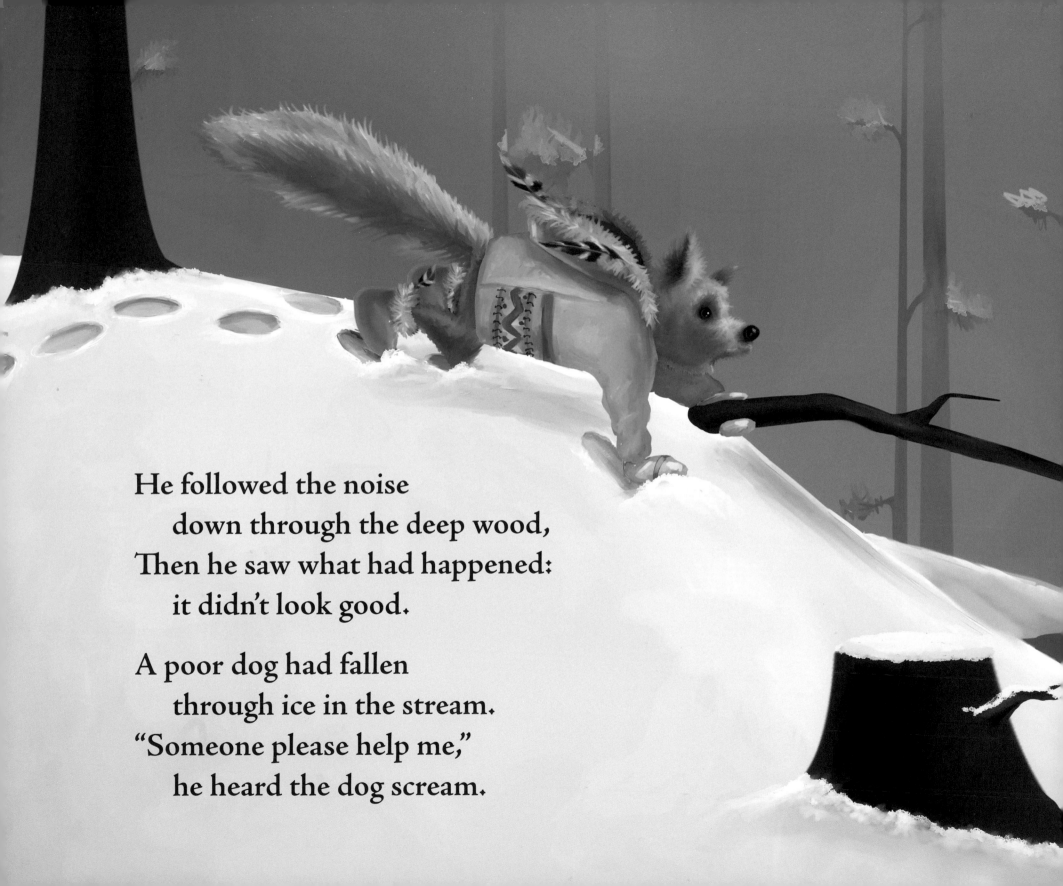

He followed the noise
    down through the deep wood,
Then he saw what had happened:
    it didn't look good.

A poor dog had fallen
    through ice in the stream.
"Someone please help me,"
    he heard the dog scream.

Without thinking he picked up
a great big long stick.
"I'll help you," cried Wolfgang.
"Grab on to this, quick!"

And he tugged and he pulled,
using all his might.
Then he saw the dog's face
and he got a big fright.

For the dog in the stream
was the very same one
Who had hurt Wolfgang's feelings
and stolen his fun.

Now the one that he'd feared
was the one he must save.
He felt scared, but would do it –
that's called being brave!

He pulled the dog out.
They both fell to the ground.
The dog's teeth started making
a chattering sound.

His body was shaking,
his face had turned blue.
He was frozen inside.
Wolfgang knew what to do.

He took off his coat
as fast as he could,
Wrapped the coat round the dog
and pulled up the hood.

Then wonderful magic began
to take place:
All the colour came back
to the frozen dog's face.

The dog had stopped shaking,
his fur was now dry.
Then to Wolfgang's surprise
he started to cry!

He said, "No one's ever
     been this nice to me.
Why do you *care?*
     You're as kind as can be!"

And deep in his eyes
     Wolfgang saw it was true
When the dog said,
     "I'm sorry, I know I hurt you."

Wolfgang was no longer
    feeling afraid:
He felt happy instead
    with the friend that he'd made.

The warmth from the love in their hearts
made them glow.
Something magic had happened
that day in the snow.

A mean dog became kind.
And a wolf understood
If you're brave and you care ...
you might find something good!